D1451284

WITHDRAWN

Dedicated to the Family

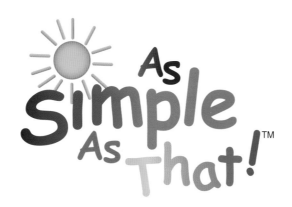

No part of this publication may be reproduced in whole or in part, or stored in a retrieval system, or transmitted in any form or by any means, electronic, mechanical, photocopying, recording or otherwise, without the written permisssion of the publisher. For information regarding permission, write to As Simple As That™, P.O. Box 31 Montauk, New York 11954.

Text and Illustrations copyright (pending) 2003 by As Simple As That™.
All rights reserved. Published by As Simple As That™.

Printed in China

Families Are Forever

An *As Simple As That*™ Story

Written by *Craig Shemin*
Based on characters by *Deb Capone*
Illustrated by *John McCoy*

HUNTINGTON CITY-TOWNSHIP
PUBLIC LIBRARY
200 W. Market Street
Huntington IN 46750

My name is Rain. I'm almost six.

Well, I'll be six soon.

Right now I'm five…and three-quarters.

And that's almost six.
That's what my mom says.

I live in a blue house with my mom and a hippo named Bo.

We live near the train. Sometimes I hear it go by.

This is my room. This is my bed.

But I didn't always live here.

I was born far, far away – in a place called China.
I don't remember much, because I was small.
Really, I don't remember much of the story at all.

But my mom told me everything – and she tells me
over and over so I don't forget.

The story still makes her cry.
It's a happy story, so I don't know why.

This is how I got here from there.

I wrote my own book and now I'll show you my story.

I started as a baby. But that was a long time ago.

I was born in China on Christmas Day.

Mom always says I was the best present she ever got.

In China, I lived in a big house with lots of other girls. An ayi (that's like a nanny) took care of me and put me to bed at night.

We were all waiting for our forever families to come and find us. I hoped and I wished that somewhere there was a forever family for me.

And somewhere, there was.

My forever mother lived in a place I had never heard of called America. She lived in a blue house near the train.

And, she had a hippo named Bo from when she was little.

Bo always sat in the window and he could see many things.

He saw the sun rise.

He saw the sun set.

He saw the seasons change.

He saw all the children with their special friends, and each time he did, he missed having his own special friend to talk to. Bo hoped that soon, someone new would join his forever family.

too many bags!

Then, one day,
the house near
the train became
very busy.
Suitcases were packed.
Diapers were stacked.
There were toys and baby things all over.
The lady who lived there was getting ready for a trip, and
getting ready for something else.

Bo could hear her talking on the telephone. She seemed to be very excited.

"It's a little girl! Isn't that wonderful? I'm going to China to bring her home."

When Bo heard her say that, he got excited, too.

bo likes flying

And soon, Bo was sitting on an airplane and enjoying the long, long, trip to China.

And after the long, long, trip Bo relaxed in the hotel and waited.

While Bo was waiting, I was riding – riding on a bus.

It was my first time on a bus.

(It was my first time anywhere!)

me

The bus was bumpy and fast, but I wasn't scared.
I had important things to think about.

"What will my family be like?" I wondered.

We finally arrived — I would soon have my forever family. And my family would have me.

first hug

A woman took me into her arms and started to cry. Holding me tight, she whispered, "I am your forever mother, starting right now."

I didn't know what to do, but since she was crying, I thought I'd cry, too.

My new Mommy hugged me and kissed me and gave me a bath. We splashed and we laughed and had a great time.

After my bath, while she was drying me off, I could see love in her eyes. So I gave it right back.

wet
head

I could see we looked different. She didn't look like anyone else I had ever known. And she didn't look like me at all.

Our eyes were different, but we could both see.
Our lips were different, but we could both smile.

My new mom tucked me in and I had one more surprise –
a soft, cuddly hippo right in front of my eyes.

I could almost hear him speak. "My name is Bo," he
whispered. "I'm also part of your family. I've known your
mom since she was a baby. That's why I'm a little worn out
around the ears. She always carried me along by my ears."

That first night with my new family, I dreamed happy dreams. I dreamed about my forever Mom, Bo and our new family. I dreamed about China.

And whatever or wherever I dreamed, Bo was right along with me, holding my hand.

"I will always be with you," he said to me. "I was always with your Mom and now we're both with you."

The next day mom told me about our house and I couldn't wait to get home. But there was a long trip ahead.

I slept on the trip, I ate and I cuddled with Bo.

I finally found my forever family.

I finally had my forever mom and my forever hippo.

But, was I surprised when the airplane landed!!

There were many more people in my new family.
I met my forever grandmother and my forever uncles and
aunts, and dozens and dozens of forever cousins.

They all cried when they saw me. I didn't know what to do, but since they were all crying, I thought I'd cry too. I can't even remember each face or each name, but they all hugged me and loved me, so I did the same.

HUNTINGTON CITY-TOWNSHIP
PUBLIC LIBRARY
200 W. Market Street
Huntington IN 46750

That's my story.
You know what
I learned?
A family is special
and each one is
different. And
some sisters and
brothers may not
look like their fathers and mothers.

But that doesn't matter, what does matter is this:
Families are forever. It's as simple as that!